A Pond Full of Pigs

A story
about the
Golden Rule

Standard
Publishing
Cincinnati, Ohio

threads™

"I think I'm ready," said Patches as he steadied himself at the end of the diving board.

"He's gonna do it!" said Rags.

"He's so brave," said Lacey.

"Be careful, Patches!" said Bobbin as he covered his eyes.

Patches jumped into the pond with a *splash*!

"Hey, what d'ya know, it's not cold at all!" said Patches. "Come on in, guys!"

Lacey and Bobbin dove in. But just as Rags started his dive, a loud horn blasted through the air. Rags belly flopped into the water.

"That horn got me all twisted up," said Rags as he got out of the pond. "I wanna find out what's making that noise. Who's with me?"

"We are!" said Lacey and Patches.

"I don't know," Bobbin said. "Adventures make me nervous."

"Aw, come on. It'll be fun," said Patches. Finally Bobbin agreed.

Patches found bees. Bobbin found clover. Rags found a rock. Lacey found a daisy. But nobody found the sound.

Finally Lacey shouted, "Look at this!" She pointed toward a hut.

"Let's get a closer look!" said Rags.

Patches, Bobbin, and Lacey all followed Rags as he headed down the hill toward the hut.

5

When they got closer to the hut, they saw a *big* horn.

"Look," said Lacey. "There's a sign." She began to read out loud: "Treat this horn as you'd treat your own. It's here for a reason, and needs to keep blowin'. Be back soon–Floyd, Pig Captain."

Suddenly the horn began to blow. It was the same sound they had heard at the pond, only louder.

"Wow!" said Rags. "I gotta get a closer look."

"Maybe it would be better to wait for Mr. Floyd to get back," said Lacey. Once again, the horn let out a loud blast.

"How about I just try and turn it down a little," said Rags. He climbed up onto the horn and began looking around.

"Do you really think you should be touching that, Rags?" asked Bobbin.

"Take it easy," said Rags. "All I wanna do is turn it down a little." As Rags touched the horn, a loud sound blasted right in his ear.

"OK, horn . . . that does it!" shouted Rags. He shook the horn. He banged on the horn. He stomped on the horn. But the horn grew louder and played faster. Desperate, Rags pulled a small valve on the horn and a piece of the valve broke off.

Suddenly the horn sputtered, coughed out a final wheeze, and then stopped.

"See, I told you I knew what I was doing," gasped Rags, as he tried to catch his breath.

From a distance came a loud splash followed by the sound of squealing pigs. Then a group of frantic fish went running past the hut.

"Pigs!" shouted a fish. "There's pigs in the pond! Somebody played with the pig horn!"

"Umm . . . that cannot be a good sign," said Bobbin.

"Aw, c'mon," said Rags. "It can't be that bad, can it?"

"Let's go and see what all this hullabaloo's about!" said Patches.

The group headed back toward the swimming hole.

When they got there, Patches let out a whistle. "Well now, that's what I call a pond full of pigs."

"No wonder the fish ran away," said Lacey. "There's no room for any-thing else!"

"Hmmm," said Rags. "Somehow, by messing with that pig horn, we must have pigged-up the pond . . . Soooo, what we need to do is *un-pig* the pond. Anybody got a plan?"

"We could try and find that Mr. Floyd," suggested Bobbin.

"Or . . . I could try roundin' those pigs up," said Patches.

"A pig roundup!" said Rags. "I love it! All right, guys, let's give him some room!"

Patches began running in a circle around the pigs. As he ran faster and faster, the pigs started to follow him. Soon Patches was just a blur, and the pigs were moving so fast, they became a giant whirlwind of pigs!

"Maybe he should *stop* rounding now," said Bobbin anxiously.

"PATCHES!" shouted Rags, Lacey, and Bobbin all together.

Patches stopped. "What?" he asked. Then one pig whacked right into Patches and he disappeared again into the giant pig whirl. When the pigs finally stopped whirling, Patches was stuck right in the middle of the pond full of pigs.

"I guess pigs don't round up so good," said Patches.

"I think we'd better go find that Pig Captain guy," said Bobbin for the second time.

"Are you kidding?" said Rags. "If he sees this, we're in big trouble."

"Maybe I could get them to leave with one of my cheers!" said Lacey. She dashed off and returned in a flash, dressed in a cheerleader outfit.

As Lacey cheered, the pigs swayed from side to side.

"I don't think this is working," said Bobbin.

"Wait, I'm not finished yet," said Lacey as she climbed up on top of the pile of pigs.

"Get outta the pond!" she cheered. "Get outta the pond . . . WAY OUT!" Then Lacey jumped and landed in the middle of the pile of pigs, right next to Patches.

"Mighty fine cheer, little lady," said Patches.

"Thank you," said Lacey.

15

"I gotta think," Rags said. "Where are my bubbles?" He pulled out a detective hat and bubble pipe and began to think hard.

"Excuse me, Rags," said Bobbin. "I hate to interrupt, but I really think we should find that Mr. Captain Floyd Pig Guy and tell him what we've done, before it gets any worse."

"Hmmm, maybe you're right, Bobbin," said Rags. But just then the bubbles coming from his pipe gave him an idea. "Wait a minute," he exclaimed. "I've got it!"

"Oh, dear," said Bobbin.

Rags blew a huge bubble. It wobbled and shimmered, and all the pigs stared at it. The bubble touched the nose of one of the pigs and—*pop*! The startled pigs jumped straight up into the sky!

"Now that's what I call unpiggin' a pond," Rags said proudly as he jumped into the empty pond. But then the pile of pigs came crashing back down to the pond and landed right on top of Rags!

"Ouch," said Rags from somewhere underneath the pigs.

"Don't panic, guys," said Bobbin. "I'm gonna find that Pig Captain and get some help!"

Just as Bobbin turned to leave, he bumped into a pig wearing overalls. "Hey, slow down, son," said the pig. "What's your hurry?"

"I gotta find the Pig Captain!" said Bobbin.

The pig smiled to himself. "Well, this is your lucky day," he said. "I'm the Pig Captain."

"You're Floyd?" said Bobbin. "Boy, am I glad to see you!"

Floyd looked around. "What happened here?" he said.

Bobbin began to explain. "Well, you see, your horn was playing really loud—"

"So Rags tried to turn it down—" interrupted Lacey.

"But he couldn't find a switch—" interrupted Patches.

"And then I kinda . . . well . . . broke it . . . a little," finished Rags. He pulled the broken piece of the horn out from the pile of pigs.

"We're really sorry," said Bobbin. "We shouldn't have even gone near it."

"I want folks to enjoy my inventions," said Floyd. "All I ask is that you treat them with a little respect. How would you like it if I broke something that belongs to you?"

"You mean like my ukulele?" asked Rags.

"Now you get the idea," said Floyd. "Let's say I borrowed your ukulele and wasn't very careful with it. What if I broke one of the strings? That would make you feel pretty bad, right?"

Rags nodded his head and said, "Just awful!"

"Well," said Floyd, "now you know how I feel about my pig horn."

Rags began to cry. "I'm sorry, Mr. Floyd, Captain, sir," he sobbed. "I'll never do anything like this again. I promise."

"Take it easy, kid," Floyd said. "Next time something like this happens, just try and remember the Golden Rule. You know, do unto others' pig horns as you would have them do unto your ukulele."

"Is that really the Golden Rule?" asked Lacey.

Floyd grinned. "Not exactly," he said. "But that's what it means."

"I remember hearing the Golden Rule," said Bobbin. "It's 'Do unto others as you would have them do unto you.' That's from the Bible."

"You betcha," said Floyd. "And it's not just about stuff, you know. It goes for people, too. You treat folks the way you want to be treated, and things will go just fine."

"Oh, thank you, Mr. Floyd," said Lacey. "That's such good advice."

"You're welcome, kid," said Floyd. "Now that's enough jaw flapping for one day. We gotta get those pigs out of that pond!"

"Just tell us what to do, Cap'n," said Patches.

Floyd scratched his head. "This is gonna be tricky," he said. "My horn's got a pig-removal song that would do the trick, but it'll take hours to get it working again."

"Hey, maybe we could sing the song," suggested Bobbin.

Floyd thought it over. "No harm in trying, I guess," said Floyd. "I'll start out and you all join in."

Floyd started singing the pig-removal song, and the others soon began to sing along. Slowly the pigs in the pile began to rise up and become less tightly packed. As Floyd, Rags, Bobbin, Patches, and Lacey continued to sing, the pigs began to move away from the pond and head toward Floyd's pigpen. When they got there, the pigs hopped into the pigpen, one on top of the other.

"What do you know, it worked!" said Floyd.

Suddenly the ground began to shake with the very loud sound of a hundred rumbling pig tummies.

"Uh, oh," said Floyd. "Sounds like they're getting hungry. I'd better get their supper. I've had enough bellyachin's for one day!" And with that, Floyd headed off to find some food for the pigs.

"Yikes, it's getting late," said Bobbin. "We'd better get going, too!"

"Wait," said Rags. "If we hurry, I've got just enough sunlight to try my dive again!" All four of them headed back to the swimming hole.

"OK, guys!" shouted Rags. "Get ready for the real triple-flipple flapjack with a cinnamon twist."

But just as Rags started his dive—

"ACHOO!" Patches sneezed so loud that Rags belly flopped into the swimming hole once again. Rags swam to the surface of the water and announced, "Tomorrow, we're going bowling!"

Everyone laughed.

Tying Up Loose Threads

Captain Floyd taught Rags and the others about the Bible's Golden Rule: "Do to others as you would have them do to you." You can read the Golden Rule in Luke 6:31.

Rags would feel bad if someone broke his favorite ukulele. So when he saw Captain Floyd's pig horn, he should have remembered the Golden Rule. Then he would have been more careful with the horn.

Would you like your friends to let you play with their toys? Share your toys with them. Do you want the kids on your street to be kind to you? Try being kind to them first. When we treat other people and their things with respect, we aren't just being nice . . . we are doing what God wants us to do!